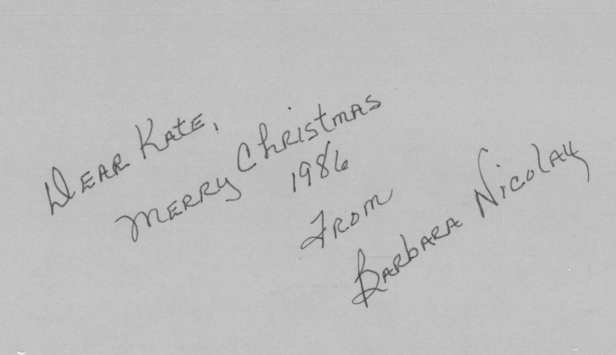

Dear Kate,
Merry Christmas
1986
From
Barbara Nicolay

THE TEDDY BEARS' PICNIC

By Jimmy Kennedy

Illustrated by Alexandra Day

A Star & Elephant Book
Green Tiger Press
La Jolla
1983

The artist wishes to thank
Rabindranath Darling and Elizabeth Ratisseau
for permitting their bears
to pose for these paintings.

Green Tiger Press
La Jolla, California 92038

ISBN 0-88138-010-5

If you go down in the woods today
You're sure of a big surprise

If you go down in the woods today
You'd better go in disguise

For every bear that ever there was

Will gather there for certain because

Today's the day the Teddy Bears have their picnic.

Every Teddy Bear who's been good
Is sure of a treat today
There's lots of marvelous things to eat
And wonderful games to play

Beneath the trees where nobody sees
They'll hide and seek as long as they please
'Cause that's the way the Teddy Bears have their picnic.

If you go down
          in the woods today

You'd better not go alone

It's lovely down
          in the woods today

But safer to stay at home

For every Bear that ever there was
Will gather there for certain because
Today's the day the Teddy Bears have their picnic.

Picnic time for Teddy Bears
The little Teddy Bears are having a lovely time today

Watch them, catch them unawares
And see them picnic on their holiday
See them gaily gad about

They love to play and shout

They never have any care

At six o'clock their mummys and daddys
Will take them home to bed

Because they're tired little Teddy Bears.

The paintings for this book were executed in egg tempera.
The type is Souvenir Light set by Eucalyptus Productions, Inc. of San Diego.
Color separations by Photolitho AG, Gossau-Zurich, Switzerland.
Printed and bound in Hong Kong.